Escape from the Twin Towers

THE RANGER IN TIME SERIES

RANGER in TIME

Escape from the Twin Towers

KATE MESSNER

illustrated by
KELLEY McMORRIS

Scholastic Inc.

Text copyright © 2020 by Kate Messner
Illustrations by Kelley McMorris, copyright © 2020 Scholastic Inc.

This book is being published simultaneously in hardcover by Scholastic Press.

Library of Congress Cataloguing-in-Publication Data
Names: Messner, Kate, author. | McMorris, Kelley, illustrator.
Title: Escape from the Twin Towers / Kate Messner ; illustrated by Kelley McMorris.
Description: New York, NY: Scholastic Inc., 2020. | Series: Ranger in time ; 11 | Summary: Ranger the time-travelling Golden retriever was trained for search-and-rescue and even though he did not pass the tests he has used his training on his many trips to help people caught up in disasters; now he has arrived at the World Trade Center on the morning of September 11, 2001 just as the first plane hits, and he must rescue fifth-graders Risha and Max who are trapped in the wreckage, guide them to safety, and hopefully reunite them with Risha's mother who works on the ninety-first floor. | Includes bibliographical references.
Identifiers: LCCN 2018060392 (print) | LCCN 2019000798 (ebook) |
ISBN 9781338538137 (Ebook) | ISBN 9781338537949 (pbk.) |
ISBN 9781338537956 (jacketed library binding)
Subjects: LCSH: World Trade Center (New York, N.Y. : 1970-2001)—Juvenile fiction. | Golden retriever—Juvenile fiction. | Time travel—Juvenile fiction. | September 11 Terrorist Attacks, 2001—Juvenile fiction. | Search and rescue operations—New York (State)—New York—Juvenile fiction. | Missing persons—Juvenile fiction. | New York (N.Y.)—History—21st century—Juvenile fiction. | CYAC: World Trade Center (New York, N.Y.: 1970-2001)—Fiction. | Golden retriever—Fiction. | Dogs—Fiction. | Time travel—Fiction. | September 11 Terrorist Attacks, 2001—Fiction. | Rescue work—Fiction. | Missing persons—Fiction. | New York (N.Y.)—Fiction.
Classification: LCC PZ7.M5615 (ebook) | LCC PZ7.M5615 Es 2020 (print) | DDC 813.6 [Fic]—dc23
LC record available at https://lccn.loc.gov/2018060392

ISBN 978-1-338-53794-9

10 9 8 7 6 5 4 3 2 1   20 21 22 23 24

Printed in the United States of America   40
First printing 2020

Book design by Ellen Duda and Stephanie Yang

Chapter 1

A Robin-Egg, Blue-Sky Morning

Risha Scott held a box of muffins and stared up at the Twin Towers. She loved visiting her mom's office at the World Trade Center. It was fun to walk through the busy, crowded plaza, with its fountain and sculpture and bright flowers. Risha loved the buzz of thousands of people, all going to work in the Twin Towers. Today she and her best friend, Max, got to spend the whole day there! They had to visit a professional workplace as part of their fifth-grade career project. Max's dad worked downtown, too, but his office didn't allow visitors.

"I call that chocolate chip muffin!" Max said as they walked into the lobby with Risha's mom. They waited to sign in at the security desk. Then they'd take the elevators up to the ninety-first floor of the North Tower, where Risha's mother worked.

Risha yawned.

"You're not tired already, are you?" her mom asked, laughing.

"You got me up so early!" Risha said as they waited for the elevator. "But I'm not complaining. Today is going to be amazing." Risha had on her navy blue dress with Mom's pretty pink-and-purple scarf tied at her neck. Mom wore the bright purple dress Risha loved, with her cool red-framed glasses and black shoes with little bows on top. Last night, Risha and Mom had even painted their fingernails the same color, a sparkly pale pink. Max was dressed up, too, wearing his dad's favorite red tie.

It was perfect September weather, with a robin's-egg-blue sky. On their way to the office, Max and Risha had gone with Mom to vote in the primary election for New York City's mayor. They'd walked another three blocks to pick up muffins for everyone in the office at the fancy bakery Risha loved. Now Risha and Max would get to help Mom at work all day.

"You know what's going to be amazing?" Max tapped a poster on the wall. It was about the Paul Taylor Dance Company's performance in the World Trade Center's outdoor plaza that night. After work, they planned to buy picnic food and stay to watch the show. Risha and Max had taken ballet lessons together when they were younger. Max was still dancing, but Risha had switched to gymnastics in fourth grade.

"That'll be you someday," Risha said, pointing to the men on the poster. She gave Max a fist bump.

"Here we go," Mrs. Scott said as the elevator doors opened. She worked on such a high floor that it took two elevators to get there! When they stepped off the second one, Risha led them down the hall to the office. Mom's company worked with big transport ships to make sure they were following rules and being safe. To be honest, Risha didn't really want to do that kind of work when she got older. She was more interested in being a gymnast and an art teacher. But missing school to spend a whole day downtown with Mom was too great a chance to pass up.

They shared the muffins, and there were a few left over. Mrs. Scott looked at her watch.

"I'm going to take a muffin down to my friend at Port Authority. You can hang out in the conference room, and I'll be right back."

She brought Risha and Max to a big room at least three times the size of Risha's bedroom. It had a long table with fancy, cushy chairs that spun around. Best of all was the wall of windows that looked out toward the Empire State Building.

"Whoa!" Max said.

Risha smiled. She'd seen the view before and was excited to share it. She pulled her colored pencils and sketchbook out of her backpack. Later, she'd need to take notes for their career project, but for now, she wanted to draw the buildings outside.

"I'll be back in a few minutes. Then I'll introduce you to some people you can interview for your project," Mom said, and closed the conference room door behind her.

"This rocks," Max said. He polished off his muffin in three bites and pulled *Harry Potter and the Goblet of Fire* from his bag.

Risha looked up from her drawing and laughed. "Haven't you already read that like three times?"

"Gets better every time," he said.

Risha went back to work on her drawing. A few minutes later, she heard a sound like an airplane. It got louder and louder. She looked out the window.

A plane was flying low in the sky. Too low! Risha stared as it roared past the Empire State Building.

It was heading straight toward them.

Chapter 2

PLAYGROUND PRACTICE

"Come on up, Ranger!" Sadie called from the top of the slide at the park. "You can do it!"

Ranger jumped onto the slide. He climbed slowly up to meet Sadie, spreading his toes so his paws wouldn't slip.

When he made it to the top, Sadie gave him a hug. "Good job!" she said. Then they slid down together.

Walking up steep slopes was something Ranger had learned in his special training with Luke and Dad. Ranger had been practicing to be a search-and-rescue dog so he could

find missing people and rescue those who needed help. Ranger had practiced following Luke's scent to find him when he was hiding in the woods. He'd practiced walking over all kinds of surfaces, including slippery slides like this one. But when it came time to take his test to be an official search-and-rescue dog, Ranger hadn't passed.

It was all because of the squirrel. In order to be a search-and-rescue dog, you had to ignore everything except the commands. You had to ignore juicy hot dog pieces and squeaky toys on the lawn. You also had to ignore squirrels. Even squirrels with big, swishy tails. Even if they ran right past while you were taking your test! That's what happened to Ranger on the day of his test. He'd chased the squirrel up a tree instead of ignoring it.

Ranger knew that Luke wasn't really missing or in trouble on the day of the test. If a real person had needed help, Ranger would have helped. But Luke was just pretending, so Ranger chased the squirrel instead.

"You sure are good at obstacles like that slide, Ranger," Luke said, scratching Ranger's neck. "Too bad you didn't pass your test. But you're still the best dog in the world." He turned to Sadie. "We should go home. Dad's making chili."

Ranger walked home alongside Luke and Sadie. When they went into the kitchen to wash up for dinner, he got a drink of water from his dish in the mudroom. Just as he was finishing, he heard a humming sound coming from his dog bed.

Ranger walked over to his bed. He pawed at his blanket until he uncovered the old first aid kit he'd dug up from Mom's garden one day. The humming was coming from the old metal box with the leather strap. And it was getting louder.

Ranger knew what that sound meant. The first aid kit only hummed when someone far away needed his help. Twice, the old metal box had taken Ranger into war zones, where young men were struggling to survive. Once, it had taken him to help two girls trapped in a trembling city full of fire and smoke. Once, it had taken him to a flooded neighborhood where people had to climb onto their roofs to keep from drowning. And now, the box was humming again.

Ranger nuzzled the first aid kit's strap over his head. The humming got louder and louder. The first aid kit grew warm at Ranger's throat. Light began to spill from the cracks. It glowed brighter and brighter. Soon it was so bright Ranger had to close his eyes. He felt as if he were being squeezed through a hole in the sky.

The humming stopped. Then a roar filled Ranger's ears. When he opened his eyes, he was standing in a room with a long table and big, cushy chairs. Next to the table was a tall window. Ranger looked out just in time to see a huge jet tip its wings.

It was enormous and close — too close! Ranger barked, and a thundering crash shook the room as the plane slammed into the building above him.

Chapter 3

TRAPPED!

Someone screamed. Parts of the ceiling caved in. A tall shelf full of binders and books tipped and slammed to the floor. Papers blew everywhere. Bits of plaster rained down on Ranger's back. He yelped and darted under a table. Another shelf came crashing down on top of the table. Ranger curled up on the carpet, trembling.

When the noise quieted, Ranger crawled out. Where was he? He stepped over jagged bits of broken wall. He could hear people somewhere down a hallway. He'd go find them.

Maybe they needed help. But just as Ranger started toward the door, he heard a muffled cough.

Ranger barked. He couldn't see anyone. But he knew that sometimes when buildings were damaged, people were trapped where they couldn't be seen. Ranger barked again to see if the person would say anything. But all he heard was the building creaking and groaning above.

Carefully, Ranger stepped through the broken furniture and ceiling tiles. Where was the person who'd coughed? Ranger sniffed the air. He smelled plaster and dust and smoke. Hot metal and melting plastic and gasoline. And then . . .

There! Ranger caught the scent of a person. Wait . . . no . . .

Two people! Ranger followed the scents to the corner of the room. That was where the first shelf had fallen on a heap of crumbled plaster. Ranger barked again, and someone called out, "Hello?"

Ranger pawed at the heavy shelf, but he couldn't move it. He had to bring help. He barked once more. Then he climbed through the debris to the door. People sounds were coming from down the hall. Ranger ran until he found some men and women huddled in a group. Ranger barked, and one of the men looked down at him.

"Whose dog is that?" he asked.

"No idea." A woman with a torn skirt shook her head. "I've seen people with service dogs, but not on this floor."

She and the man both turned away. Ranger barked again. He pawed at the man's leg. When the man looked, Ranger ran down the hall toward the room where the ceiling had fallen. He stopped and barked again. Then he raced to the man, and back down the hall. Back and forth Ranger ran, barking and barking.

The woman with the torn skirt gasped. "Were Sudha's daughter and her friend down there?"

She and the man followed Ranger down the hall and into the battered conference room.

"Hello?" the woman called. "Risha! Are you here?"

Ranger climbed back to the spot where he'd heard the cough. He barked, and a weak voice called out, "We're here . . ."

"Hold on!" the woman shouted. "We're going to get you out!"

Risha couldn't see anything from under the rubble, but she recognized the woman's voice. It was her mother's friend, Mrs. Burt, who worked in the reception area. "We're all right!" Risha called. "But we can't move."

"It's okay. Just sit tight . . ." The man began pulling tiles and pieces of wall from the pile. He tried to lift the big shelf but couldn't.

"We need strong arms down here!" he shouted out the door. Soon, two other men came rushing in to help.

"Easy now," one of them said. "On three. One . . ."

The men bent down and wrapped their hands under the edge of the shelf.

"Two . . . three!"

Together, they lifted the heavy shelf. A pink-nail-polished hand burst up from the plaster and dust.

"There she is!" Mrs. Burt grabbed Risha's hand and pulled her carefully out of the mess.

Max crawled out behind her, coughing. Then he sat back and looked at Ranger. "That dog found us." He leaned over and lifted the first aid kit from Ranger's neck. "And he brought . . . bandages and stuff?"

"That dog wouldn't leave us alone until we came for you," the man from the other room said. "You sure you're all right?"

"I'm okay," Max said, and then looked at Risha. "You've got a big scrape on your forehead." He took a bandage from Ranger's first aid kit.

"I'll be okay," Risha said as Max put the bandage on for her. "But I need to find my mom."

Mrs. Burt's eyes darted to the other adults. Her face was full of concern. "Where did she go?"

"She . . ." Risha's breath caught in her throat. The morning came rushing back. The low-flying airplane. The crash and the dust and the darkness. The plane must have slammed into the building above them.

Where had Mom said she was bringing those muffins? Had she taken the elevator upstairs? What if she was where the plane had hit? Risha's eyes burned with tears.

Max answered for her. "She said she was going to Port Authority."

Mrs. Burt let out her breath. "That's way down on the sixty-eighth floor." She put a hand around Risha's shoulders. "Your mama's fine. She's probably already —" She broke out coughing before she could finish her sentence. The smoke was getting thicker. When Mrs. Burt stopped coughing, she looked at Risha. "We'll find your mom outside. Right now, we all need to get out of this building."

Chapter 4

NINETY-ONE FLOORS TO GO

Everyone rushed to the office reception area. Outside the window, thousands of pieces of paper fluttered down from above. They looked like giant white butterflies in the wind. Inside, the smoke was getting thicker.

A woman gave Risha and Max bottles of water and wet paper towels. "For your nose and mouth," she said, hurrying on to the next people.

Max was still holding Ranger's first aid kit. "Should we bring this?"

Risha nodded. "Here . . ." She grabbed her

backpack and tucked the first aid kit and water inside.

Risha and Max didn't have cell phones, but lots of other people were making calls. Their voices spilled together.

"Hank, is that you?"

"Yes, it was an airplane. We don't know anything more."

"Heading down now. I'll call when I'm out."

"Does your mother have her phone?" Mrs. Burt asked Risha as she held out her own.

"I'm not sure," Risha said, but she took it and dialed. It went right to a fast busy signal. "The call didn't go through."

Mrs. Burt sighed. "Lines are all tied up. It's okay. We'll meet up with her outside."

A man came running in from the hallway. "We found a way down! Two stairways are blocked, but the other one is clear. We've got to go now. Follow me!"

Ranger walked between Risha and Max as they felt their way through the smoky hallway. At the door to the stairs, everyone stopped. It was pitch-black. Fire alarms echoed through the emptiness. Someone behind them turned on a flashlight.

Risha stood on her tiptoes so she could see. The sprinkler system must have gone off. Water was cascading down the stairs from above.

"Careful!" someone shouted. "It's going to be slippery!"

The woman in front of Risha wore a bright blue blouse. Risha tried to focus on that instead of her pounding heart as she stepped into the dark staircase.

Follow the blue, she thought as they started down the first flight of stairs. *Follow the blue*.

Ranger walked just behind Risha, in front of Max. He was glad they were leaving this

place. The stairwell smelled hot and danger-
ous, like smoke and sweat and fuel. It burned
his nose and throat. Where was the fresh air?

Two flights down, emergency lights flick-
ered on. Risha was grateful. But just as she
relaxed her grip on the railing, she slipped.

"Risha!" Max grabbed her arm just in time
to keep her from tumbling down the whole
flight of stairs. "Are you okay?" he asked as she
scrambled to her feet.

"I'm all right," Risha said. But she'd banged
her knee hard. She wished she could sit and
put ice on it, but they had to keep going. The
smoke was getting thicker. Mom would be
waiting for them downstairs. She'd be wor-
ried. Risha tried to count the floors as she
followed the blue-blouse lady down.

Eighty-six . . . eighty-five . . . eighty-four . . .

Before long, the stream of people stopped.
Risha stood sweating in the staircase, waiting

to move again. But then word came up from below. Something was blocking the stairwell. They'd have to find another way down. Risha followed the crowd into a hallway. She'd lost count of what floor they were on. She and Max trailed after the woman in blue through the smoke until they found another staircase and started the long march down again.

Follow the blue . . . Follow the blue . . .

Ranger stayed close to Risha. He was afraid she might slip again. Every once in a while, he felt her hand on his back. He did his best to be still and strong, to steady her. The staircase was so crowded. There were so many smells! And so many voices.

"Stay to the right!" someone shouted. Risha looked behind her. Two men were helping an injured woman down the steps. She had terrible burns on her face and arms. But she was walking calmly down the stairs, eyes ahead.

Risha swallowed hard. She'd thought she and Max were unlucky to be trapped when the plane hit. Now she understood. They were the lucky ones.

When they reached the seventy-first floor, Risha called to Max, "Can you get that water?" She paused so he could unzip her backpack. Max pulled out the two water bottles and handed her one. It was warm, but it felt good in her dusty throat. The staircase was so hot, and they had so far left to go. Risha leaned down and gave Ranger a quick drink, too.

Max wiped sweat from his forehead. He pulled off his necktie. "Okay if I shove this in your bag?" he asked. Risha nodded. He zipped it into her backpack, and they started down again.

Sixty-one . . . sixty . . . fifty-nine . . .

Soon, Risha told herself, they'd be out in the plaza. Mom would be waiting. Everything would be all right.

"Move aside!" someone shouted as they approached the forty-fifth floor. A long line of firefighters was coming up. The stairs were so narrow that Risha and Max had to turn sideways to make room for them.

Risha watched the firefighters pass, red-faced and breathing hard. It was so tiring climbing down all these stairs. She couldn't imagine climbing up. And with all that gear! The firefighters carried axes and hoses, and tanks of air on their backs. They wore heavy, dark coats with bright yellow markings, and had serious looks on their faces.

How many people were still upstairs? Those firefighters had to know what it was like on the higher floors. But they were going into the smoke and darkness anyway. They were rushing in as everyone else ran away.

Chapter 5

ESCAPE FROM THE NORTH TOWER

Risha stared as the firefighters climbed past her. She hoped her mom had already left the building. But just in case she hadn't — just in case she was up there somewhere — Risha felt grateful someone was going up to help.

"Thank you," she said as the firefighters passed. Other people started saying it, too.

"Thank you for your service."

"Be careful up there."

"We'll be praying for you."

One of the firefighters, a man with bushy brown hair sticking out from under his hat, paused to catch his breath on the step opposite Risha. She stopped, too, and held out her water bottle. He hesitated, but then took it and had a drink.

"Thank you," he said, handing it back. He gave Ranger a quick pat on the head. "Go on now. You need to keep moving." He started climbing again.

"Be safe!" Risha called after him.

"You too," he said, and disappeared up the next set of stairs.

The line of firefighters went on and on. Risha had counted more than a hundred by the time she and Max reached the twentieth floor. She couldn't imagine how the firefighters were carrying so much heavy equipment. Her backpack couldn't weigh more than five or ten pounds, but her back was soaked with sweat. She'd run out of water ten floors ago. Her throat was sore and dry. Her feet were wet, and her fancy city shoes pinched her toes with every step.

Behind her, Max coughed. He'd been coughing more and more as they descended.

Risha looked over her shoulder. "You doing okay?"

Max nodded, but his eyes were watering. "Wish I had my inhaler. It's in my bag back in the conference room."

Ranger gave a quiet bark. A gap in the line had opened in front of Risha when she slowed down. Ranger nudged her with his nose. He didn't like this long, crowded stairway. They needed to get outside where there was fresh air, where things didn't feel so shaky and dangerous. They needed to find Risha's mother, so Risha and Max could go home. Maybe then Ranger could go home, too.

Finally, they approached a landing where an open door led to a bright mezzanine. Risha had never been so relieved to see sunlight. She hurried down the last few steps. Mom would be waiting on the plaza outside. She'd hug them and tell them how grown up they'd been. She'd tell them how proud she was.

"We made it!" Risha said. But when she stepped into the light, her relief turned to horror.

"Don't look!" someone shouted. "Don't look outside!"

But it was too late. Risha couldn't look away.

The beautiful, flower-filled plaza — the one where they were supposed to watch the dance performance tonight — was covered in burning, twisted metal. Whatever had fallen from the sky had crushed the pretty fountain and sculpture. All around, charred papers, dust, and hunks of concrete littered the sidewalks where people should have been.

"Keep moving!" a firefighter shouted.

"Risha, let's go!" Max said. But she felt frozen to the ground.

Ranger barked. He licked Risha's hand, but she kept staring out the window. People streamed past them. Some people started crying and running. A man tripped and stumbled into Risha. Another man pushed past him. The march down the stairs had felt orderly and mostly calm, but now the lobby was full of panic and fear. Ranger had to get Risha and Max out of that building before they got trampled.

Ranger barked again. He jumped up on Risha and knocked her off-balance so that she stumbled a little. Max caught her arm and turned her away from the window. "Risha, come on!" he said. "We have to go!"

"This way!" a firefighter shouted, pointing to a stalled escalator.

Risha swallowed hard and nodded. She

kept a hand on Ranger as they went down the steps and through a concourse to a big mall underneath the towers. Risha's mom had brought her here just a month ago to shop for school clothes at the Gap. Now store windows were smashed, and the floor was covered in dirty water from the sprinklers raining down on everyone.

Risha looked around for her mother's coworkers, but the lady in the blue shirt was nowhere to be found. She didn't recognize anyone at all. She and Max were on their own.

Up ahead, a woman held up a bright yellow umbrella as she walked through the mall in the smelly sprinkler rain. It almost made Risha laugh. She couldn't imagine worrying about wet hair at this point. But then she realized everyone was following that yellow umbrella through the mess. Police officers were directing people the same way. Maybe

the lady wasn't trying to stay dry at all. Risha fixed her eyes on the yellow umbrella and kept walking.

"This way!" A police officer pointed to a set of stalled escalators. "When you get outside, keep moving, and don't look up!"

Keep moving. Don't look up. Keep moving . . .

Risha and Max were halfway to the escalators when a rumble shook the shopping mall.

Max stopped and grabbed Risha's hand as it grew louder. "What is that?"

Before Risha could answer, a great cloud of dust and wind burst into the concourse. In an instant, everything went black.

Chapter 6

DARKNESS AND DUST

The blast swept Risha off her feet, slammed her into the wall, and knocked all the air from her chest. When she tried to breathe, thick, bitter dust packed into her mouth. It filled her nose and scratched her eyes. She couldn't hear out of one ear. In the other, she heard only the wind and screams.

"Hold your breath!" someone shouted.

Risha's lungs burned. She pulled her mother's scarf up over her mouth and tried to breathe through that. But it was too late to keep the sharp dust from burning her throat.

Risha couldn't breathe. She couldn't see anything. Not Max or the dog. Not even her own hands in front of her. She curled into a ball and squeezed her eyes closed. How long could a person go without breathing? She didn't think she could last much longer.

But then, the roar of the wind died down. Risha heard a muffled bark.

She spit out a mouthful of thick dust. She coughed and choked out a single word. "Dog?"

The blast of wind and dust had thrown Ranger into a corner. He'd crouched against the cracked wall of a clothing store. His paws stung. His mouth and nose were so coated with dust that it was hard to smell anything at all. But he'd heard Risha's voice. He had to get the kids out of here. Ranger could feel it in his paws. This loud, dusty, trembling place wasn't safe at all.

He stood up and tried to shake off some of

the dust. It clung to his fur like mud. It was too dark to see. Ranger sneezed twice. Soot flew out of his nose, but it was still impossible to smell anything except dust and chemicals and smoke. Where were Risha and Max?

Ranger barked again. He stood still and listened.

All around him, people were coughing, crying out, calling to one another. Glass shattered nearby. Footsteps crunched over it. And then — again — a quiet voice.

"Dog? Are you here? Max? Where are you?"

The voice had come from up ahead, where Ranger thought the escalators had been. He sneezed again and sniffed the air. It was still thick with dust. It was different from anything Ranger had ever smelled. This dust seemed to be made of everything — ashes and concrete, furniture and clothing and things too awful to think about. It burned his eyes and throat.

But Ranger kept sniffing as he circled the area. Finally, there were people smells, too — live people, who smelled like smoke and sweat and fear. None of them were people Ranger knew until he turned a corner.

There! In the dark, thick air he caught the scent of the Risha girl. Ranger barked.

Her voice was closer now. "Dog? I'm here!"

Ranger found her curled on the floor and nuzzled her face. Risha sat up, threw her arms around him, and pulled him close.

Ranger was grateful for the love, but there was no time to snuggle. He had to get Risha out of the building. He pulled away and pawed at her until she stood up. She didn't seem to be badly hurt.

"Anybody over here?" a woman's voice called out.

"I am!" Risha answered. She waved her hand into the darkness until it landed on someone's sleeve.

"Come with me," the woman said. She flicked on a flashlight and held Risha's arm. "We need to get out to the street."

Risha pulled her arm away. All around her, people she couldn't see were crying and coughing. Max was here somewhere. She couldn't leave him. "I have to find my friend first. He was just with me. He has asthma."

"Oh, my dear girl . . ." The woman's voice was sad and scared. "We need to leave that to the rescue workers. We have to evacuate — now."

Risha stepped away into the dark. "Max!" she called out. Her throat was scratched and sore, but she forced herself to be louder. "Max!"

Ranger rushed to Risha's side. He leaned against her so she would know he was there. He wanted to help Max, too. But his whole

body was prickling. Even in the dark, wet dust, this place had a hot, unstable feeling to it. He wanted to get out. But not without Risha's friend.

"Oh, dog!" Risha sank to her knees and hugged his neck. "We have to find Max!"

Chapter 7

RESCUE IN THE RUINS

Find? Ranger barked.

"You know that word? Find?"

Ranger barked again. *Find!*

Risha gasped. She'd seen television shows about search-and-rescue dogs who smelled a shirt or scarf or something and then ran off to find the person who'd left it behind. She didn't know where this lost golden retriever had come from, but he had that first aid kit. Maybe he was one of those dogs. Maybe he could find Max so they could get out of this awful place.

Please, Risha thought. The woman with the flashlight had gone, and it was too dark to see. But she took off her backpack and unzipped it. She felt around until she touched the smooth fabric of the tie Max had taken off in the stairwell. She found Ranger's face with her hand and held the tie to his nose.

"That's Max's tie," she said. "He's here somewhere. Can you find him?"

Ranger sniffed at the tie. It smelled like smoke from the stairs, chocolate chip muffin crumbs and sweat and Risha's friend. But there were so many scents pooling in this dark, dusty, closed-in place. Ranger had never smelled so many awful things at once. He'd never found someone in a place like this. He wasn't sure if he could. But he knew he had to try.

Ranger moved closer to Risha until he felt

her hand on his collar. He couldn't lose her, too. Slowly, he walked through the darkness, sniffing the air. He smelled smoke and hot metal and the awful everything-dust. He smelled people — so many people! But none of them were Max.

Above them, the building groaned and rumbled. Ranger heard frightened voices, shuffling footsteps, and coughs. He sniffed the air again.

There!

It was faint, but he was certain he'd smelled it. The Max smell from the tie!

Ranger followed the scent around a wet heap of fallen-down ceiling tiles. There was a cough, and a high-pitched wheeze.

"Max!" Risha shouted. "Max? Is that you?"

"Here . . ." His voice was barely a whisper, but it was enough. Risha dropped to her hands

and knees in the soggy dust and crawled until she found him. His breath sounded ragged and choked.

Risha took his hand. "You're having an asthma attack," she said. Somehow, she made her voice calm. Helping someone else was easier than thinking about herself. "Try to relax. You have to get up. We have to get out of here." She helped Max to his feet and stood blinking into the dark.

Now what?

Risha didn't know where to go, but they had to move, so she started shuffling forward. She wished she could hold on to the dog's collar, but she couldn't do that and support Max, too. The dog brushed against her leg every few steps, though. He wouldn't leave them. Risha understood that somehow. She still didn't know where he'd come from. He wasn't their dog, but he'd decided that they were his, at least for today.

"Does anyone know where to go?" Risha called into the dark.

"Here!" called a woman's voice. "Hold on . . ." In a few seconds, Risha felt a hand on her arm. "Put your hands on my shoulders and follow," the woman said. "We've made a chain of people. There's a police officer up front who knows the complex."

Risha put one hand on the woman's shoulder ahead of her. She kept her other arm around Max.

Little by little, they felt their way to another broken escalator. Risha clung to the railing as they climbed, step by dusty step. At the top, she found the woman's shoulder again. She pulled Max to stand beside her. His breathing was shallow and fast.

"You doing okay?" she asked.

Max didn't answer, but he squeezed her hand.

"We're on our way out," Risha said. "Everything's going to be okay."

With each step, she felt Max leaning harder against her. "You're going to be all right," she said. But she didn't know if it was a promise she'd be able to keep.

Chapter 8

FIGHTING FOR BREATH

Ranger walked beside Max as they shuffled through the darkness. His nose was full of dust and smoke again, but finally there was another smell. Outdoor air!

Ranger barked. It was coming from off to one side — not where the woman was leading Risha.

Ranger stopped. Max paused beside him. Risha stopped, too, and the people who had joined the human chain behind her all bumped into one another.

Ranger barked again. He pawed at Risha.

Then he leaned his body against her, pushing her toward the outdoor-air smell.

"Wait!" Risha called to the woman in front of her. "The dog . . ." She didn't know what to say. This random dog that we just met wants us to go the other way? But that felt right. "He's telling us there's an exit over here!"

Ranger barked again. "Good dog," Risha said, and turned in the direction he was nudging her. "Let's go!" She felt Ranger at her side with every step as they shuffled through the darkness. "This way!" She felt Max's weight against her and the woman's hand on her shoulder as they trudged through the dust.

It wasn't long before Risha saw a clouded, dim light. She wanted to run, but the closer they got to the light, the more debris blocked their way. They had to duck under a section of sagging ceiling tiles and wires.

"Out this way!" a deep voice called. Up

ahead, a dust-covered police officer stood by an open door that led outside. As Risha approached, his radio crackled to life.

"Be advised," a staticky voice said. "The remaining tower is leaning to the southwest at this time. It appears to be buckling in the southwest corner."

The remaining tower? Risha couldn't stop to think about what that meant. She stepped up to the door. The police officer took her hand. His voice was urgent. "Head for the stairs and get down to the street as fast as you can." Risha met his eyes. They were red and puffy and haunted. "Don't look up. Just go."

She nodded and stepped outside. She wanted to run, but she knew Max wasn't up to it, and she couldn't lose him. Not now. All around them, people raced for the stairs that led from the raised plaza down to the street to safety. She tried to pull Max just a little faster, but he doubled over. He couldn't breathe.

No! Not now, Risha thought. Not here with glass and burning paper and terrible things falling all around them.

"Does anybody have an inhaler?" she shouted.

"Here!" Someone threw something blue at her. Risha caught it. It was an inhaler like the one Max used. Risha looked for the person who had thrown it, but they were gone.

"Max, here!" She held it to his mouth. Max's eyes widened. He took it and managed two quick puffs. He held his breath and bent over again.

Come on. Come on, Risha thought as people ran past them. But all she said to Max was, "It's okay. You're going to be okay."

Ranger leaned against Max. He couldn't help the boy breathe, but he could let him know he wasn't alone. Ranger did that for Luke sometimes, too. When Luke was sick or sad or afraid, Ranger would stay extra close. It helped.

But Ranger knew they couldn't wait here much longer. No matter how tired and sick Max was, they had to move. He barked and pawed at Risha's leg.

She looked at Ranger. Then she took Max's hand. "We have to go, Max. We can't wait." Max was still wheezing, but he let Risha lead him across the plaza toward the stairs that led down to the street.

The stairs were crowded with people. Their faces were streaked with sweat and blood and the awful dust that wouldn't go away. Some people were panicking, pushing their way forward. Ranger stayed close to Risha and Max and tried to keep people from bumping them.

At the bottom of the stairs, they were swept

up in a river of people flowing down the street. Risha scanned the crowd for her mother but couldn't find her. So she just kept walking with the crowd. Rumors swirled through the air with the dust.

"Rescue boats . . ."

"Head for the river."

"Another airplane . . ."

"Terrorists . . ."

"If the second tower falls . . ."

Risha stopped. If the *second* tower falls?

Risha knew she shouldn't look up, but she couldn't help it. She had to see for herself. She turned and looked, but there was only an empty space in the sky where the South Tower should have been. She understood now what had made that awful explosion of wind and dust back in the shopping mall.

It was gone. The South Tower was gone.

The North Tower — the one they'd just

climbed down — stood alone, and it was on fire, with angry black smoke pouring from a gash near the top of the building.

As Risha stared, the top of the tower began to sink. For a second, it looked as if the whole tower were melting into the ground. Then it buckled. The antenna toppled, and the whole sky roared as the building collapsed on itself. One floor after another came crashing down, steel on steel, crushing everything below.

Risha stared as the tower disappeared. It vanished into an enormous cloud of gray dust that raced out from its base. Then someone grabbed her hand and shouted.

"Run!"

Chapter 9

RACE TO SHELTER

Risha took Max's hand and pulled him up the street. She glanced back for just a second. The roaring cloud of dust looked like a tornado churning toward them. It was moving fast. Too fast for Max to outrun. They had to find shelter. But where?

Risha tried the door to an apartment building. It was locked. But next door, there was a little shop with snacks and souvenirs. Risha yanked open the door and pulled Max inside.

Ranger pushed in behind them, nudging them farther into the store. He could feel the earth shaking under his paws. It wasn't safe to be near the door.

A second later, the cloud of dust and debris blasted up the street, and everything went dark. Something slammed into the shop's door, and the glass shattered. Risha huddled with Max and Ranger. Someone screamed, and she realized they weren't the only ones who'd taken shelter there.

When the wind stopped and the dust began to clear, Risha opened her eyes. Half a dozen office workers huddled in the back of the store. Their suits and dresses were caked with dust.

"Were you in the North Tower?" a woman asked Risha.

Risha nodded. "You too?"

"Sixty-eighth floor."

Risha's heart sped up. That was Port Authority, where her mother's friend worked.

Where her mother had taken the muffins. "Do you know a woman named Sudha Scott?"

The woman shook her head. "I'm sorry."

"That's okay," Risha said. But it wasn't. Nothing was okay.

Max stood up and tugged on Risha's arm. "Come on," he said. His breathing had gotten better, but his voice was ragged and hoarse. "If they were on the same floor as your mom, they would have evacuated around the same time. I bet she's close by."

Risha stood up and started for the door.

"Wait," the woman said. "Your mother works at Port Authority?"

"No." Risha turned. "She works on the ninety-first floor. We were at her office, but she went down to bring her friend a muffin and then . . ." Risha stopped.

The morning flashed through her mind. The plane and the crash. The dust and the stairs and the darkness. She swallowed hard. "And then we had to evacuate and we don't know where she is."

The woman looked at her coworkers. "That must have been Cindy's friend. With the bakery box." She looked back at Risha. "I saw her."

"You did?" Risha's heart filled with hope. Finally, someone could help them! "Do you know where she was going? Was she ahead of you or behind you when you left?"

"I don't know where she is now," the woman said. "She didn't evacuate with us. As soon as the explosion happened — we didn't know then it was an airplane — she said she had to get back upstairs."

"No," Risha whispered. Mom had gone back upstairs to find Risha and Max. Of course she had. She would never leave without them. But they'd left without her. And now she was . . .

Risha squeezed her eyes closed against the

thought. She felt all the bitter dust that had filled the air settle in her stomach. She sank to the floor in the middle of a heap of Empire State Building souvenirs that had fallen from the shelves, and she cried.

She felt Max's hand on her shoulder. "Risha," he said. "It's gonna be okay. She probably got back right after we left. She'd have found the office empty and gone downstairs. I bet she was right behind us. She made it out, too. I know she did."

Risha forced herself to listen. She wiped her tear-streaked face with her scarf. Her mother's scarf.

Slowly, Risha stood up. Her mother had to be all right. She had to be. Risha wouldn't let herself imagine anything else.

The woman from the sixty-eighth floor took Risha's hand. "You should stay with us for now. We'll help you find her." She pulled a cell phone from her pocket. "Have you tried calling already?"

Risha nodded. "It wouldn't go through." But she took the phone and dialed her mother's number. This time, the phone rang.

Please. Please. Please! Risha thought.

It rang four more times, and then Risha heard her mother's cheery voice mail message. "Hi, this is Sudha. I'm not available right now . . ." Risha waited for it to finish and then said, "Mom, it's me. We're safe. We're out of the building, and I . . . I hope you're okay." Risha's throat tightened. She didn't know what else to say. But she remembered her family's safety plan at home. If there were ever a fire in their apartment, they'd meet at the coffee shop on the corner. "If you get this message, you should meet us at the bakery where we got the muffins this morning." She handed the phone back.

"Is there someone else we can call?" the woman asked. "To come get you?"

"My dad," Max said, and they dialed his number. This time, they got the fast busy signal again.

"Would you like me to take you to the police?" the woman asked. "They might be able to get through to someone."

Risha shook her head. She needed her mom. She needed to know that her mom was okay. Her mom would check her phone and she'd be proud of Risha for thinking of a meeting place, just like their emergency plan. "We're going to go wait for my mom where I told her." She looked at Max, who nodded.

"But thank you," Risha told the woman. She brushed the broken glass off her knees and walked out the door.

Chapter 10

SHOES IN THE ASHES

Ranger walked between Risha and Max as they made their way up the street. The air smelled like fire and dust and metal. And people! There were so many people, crying and shouting in all different languages. The one thing all their voices had in common was fear. Some people were running. Some walked in a daze as if they were lost. Some had their arms around friends who were hurt.

Max was doing better now, but Risha still listened to his breathing as they walked. She looked up at the sky, and the papers that fluttered down to the sidewalk, some of them charred or even in flames. Was her drawing of the city skyline up there somewhere, swirling through the smoke?

Risha tripped over a briefcase and remembered to watch her step. They were walking through soot up to their ankles, past twisted fire trucks and smoldering cars. The air was full of coughing and crying and sirens. People hurried along with neckties and paper towels pressed to their faces. Risha searched the crowd for her mother's purple dress. A woman in a polka-dot shirt was helping a man with burns on his arms. An older woman in a flowered dress limped down the sidewalk with one shoe on and one off. Two men — one young and one older — walked side by side, holding hands. But her mother was nowhere in the crowd.

Someone grabbed Risha's arm from behind. She jumped and turned.

"What floor were you on?" a woman asked. Her dress was burned at the hem, and her eyes were wild.

"Ninety-one," Risha said, and the woman ran off in tears. Risha looked at Max, confused.

Max understood. "She's looking for someone who was up higher than that."

Risha's heart sank for the woman, for everyone who'd been on the floors above them. It broke for everyone who was searching for those people now, hoping the way she was. Risha put a hand on Ranger's head.

Ranger felt the sadness in her touch. He didn't stop walking, but he leaned into her a little more. When she took her hand away, he nuzzled her fingers until she looked down at him. She smiled just a little and stroked his fur.

Risha took a shaky breath. She had to keep hoping. She had to keep telling herself that

Mom would get her message. They'd wait at the bakery, and she would come. Maybe she was already there.

Risha tried to move a little faster, but she tripped again. The pavement was covered with smoking pieces of metal and jagged chunks of broken glass. Risha's eyes fell on a pair of reading glasses. They had black frames — not red like her mother's. There were charred file folders and papers with singed edges. A hairbrush. A suitcase.

And shoes. So many high-heeled shoes, all covered in the awful gray dust. Risha hoped the women wearing them had kicked them off on purpose. There were lots of black shoes, but none of them had bows on the front.

Finally, Max and Risha turned down the street with the little bakery. It was closed and locked, but that didn't matter. There were

other people standing around at the corner, as if they were looking for someone, too. Risha searched the crowd. Her mother wasn't there.

"What do you want to do?" Max asked.

"We have to wait," Risha said. "She'll come. As soon as she gets the message, she'll come." Risha tried to sound certain when she said it, like there was no way anything else could happen. Like there was no other way the day could end.

She and Max sat down on the sidewalk. They leaned against the cool bricks of the bakery wall. A man was passing out water bottles from an abandoned bagel cart in the street. Risha and Max shared one. They rinsed the gray dust from their mouths and each had a long drink. Risha gave Ranger a drink, too. She wet her scarf and used it to wipe the ash from Ranger's eyes and nose. "There," she said. "Is that better?"

Ranger leaned against her and let her stroke his matted fur. He was glad Risha and Max were safe for now. But when would Risha's mother come to find them? And when would he get to go home?

Chapter 11

SADNESS AND SCARVES

Mom will be here soon, Risha told herself as she watched the stream of people on the street. *She'll be here soon.*

"Do you kids need a phone?" a man in an apron asked, holding out his.

"Thank you." Risha took it and tried her mother. The call went through, but then went to voice mail — again. She didn't leave another message. She handed the phone to Max. He dialed and waited.

"Dad?" he said, and his face lit up. "I'm okay. We're both fine. We're at this bakery waiting for Risha's mom." He listened. Then he said, "No . . ." and "We don't know." Max swallowed hard. He listened for a long time and then said, "Okay . . . yeah. Okay . . . We'll find you there. Love you, too." He handed the phone to the man in the apron. "Thanks." Then he turned to Risha. "Dad says they just issued an evacuation order for Lower Manhattan. So . . . we can't stay here. And he can't get to us. They've blocked off the streets. But he says there are boats taking people across the river. He'll meet us down there."

Max stood up and held out his hand. Risha didn't take it. She shook her head. "I have to wait here for my mom." She stared into the empty sky where the towers used to be. Smoke still rose from the ruins, but otherwise there were no clouds at all. How could the sky still be blue? Didn't it know what had happened?

Risha couldn't leave. As long as she stayed

here, she could believe her mom was about to walk down the street. Walking to the river with Max felt like giving up. It felt like accepting that her worst fears might be true, even if she didn't say them aloud.

Risha shook her head again. "You go ahead. I'm staying. I have to."

The man in the apron knelt down beside them. "An evacuation order means that the police will be here soon. They'll clear everybody out. Your mom, too. Best to go now with your friend. You can find his dad, and then you can all meet up later on."

Someone blew a whistle, and Risha looked up. Two police officers were walking down the street. They were talking with people and pointing toward the Hudson River. The man was right. Risha didn't have a choice. But she still felt like she was leaving her mother behind.

Risha buried her face in her mother's scarf. Even with everything that had happened — the evacuation and the smoke and the dust — she could smell her mother's perfume.

Ranger leaned against Risha and put his paw on her knee. He sniffed at the scarf, too. It smelled like smoke and sweat, like flowers and Risha and like someone else, too.

Risha looked up at him, her eyes wide. The dog had found Max in the dark after the dust storm in the shopping mall just by sniffing his tie. Risha took off the scarf and held it out to Ranger. He sniffed it again and looked up at her.

"That's Mom's scarf," she said. "My mom. Can you find her like you did Max? Can you find my mom?"

"The mayor has issued an evacuation order for Lower Manhattan!" an approaching officer called out. "Everybody needs to head for the

river!" He stopped beside Risha and Max and the man in the apron. "Are you their father?"

The man shook his head. "But they can come with me."

"My dad is meeting us at the river," Max said.

A woman in a green dress and dusty sneakers stepped up to them. She looked like somebody's mom. She must have been listening, too. "We can all go together. Come on now." She reached down. Risha took her hand and stood up. She was going to have to evacuate with everyone else. She'd have to leave now. But the dog could stay.

Risha knelt down, put an arm around Ranger, and hugged him tight. She held the scarf out once more. Ranger sniffed it again and barked.

"Please, dog," Risha whispered. "Find my mom."

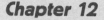

Chapter 12

SEARCH FOR SURVIVORS

Ranger watched as Risha and Max walked away with the man in the apron and the woman in the green dress. They'd be safe now. Ranger understood that. But his first aid kit was still in Risha's backpack. It hadn't made a sound. That meant his job wasn't done.

Ranger sniffed the air as he walked back up the street. He smelled dust and smoke and lots of people. But there was no mom scent from the scarf. Not yet.

As people in business suits streamed past him in one direction, firefighters rushed by in the other. Ranger followed them back into the smoke. They were gathering at the edge of an enormous mountain of beams and concrete and shattered glass. Ranger stood in the middle of the rescue workers and stared out at the pile.

He didn't know where Risha's mom was, but he was good at finding people. In his search-and-rescue training with Luke and Dad, he'd practiced finding people in all kinds of places. He'd found Luke when Luke was hiding behind dead trees. He'd found him when Luke was crouched in barrels and half-buried in the snow. Ranger had searched wide open meadows and tangly woods. He'd searched old buildings and warehouses full of crates and boxes. But he'd never seen anything like this.

"Here, dog!" one of the firefighters called quietly, slapping his knee. Ranger trotted over to him. The man reached down and pulled Ranger close, stroking his fur as he listened to an officer call out orders.

"Is that dog part of a K-9 search team?" someone asked. "Where's his handler, Tom?"

Tom the firefighter shrugged and looked down at Ranger. "No clue. He doesn't even have a harness. Seems ready to go, though. I can take him onto the pile." He gave Ranger a scratch on the neck, and his eyes teared up. "Come on, boy. I've got a lot of friends down in this mess. Let's find 'em."

Find! Ranger looked up at Tom and wagged his tail.

"You're ready, aren't you?" For a second, Tom almost smiled. "Come on, boy," he said, and together they headed toward the massive pile of rubble.

The whole block was buried in crumbled slabs of concrete and twisted steel. When the towers came down, everything was mangled and packed together. But there were still spaces in between. Ranger had learned that in his search-and-rescue training with Luke and Dad. There were always spaces. And where there were spaces, there might be survivors.

The rescue workers walked slowly through the ruins. They carried hoses to fight the flames that occasionally licked up from the pile. They carried axes in case they found someone trapped.

Tom took a careful step onto a beam that shifted under his boots. "Watch this spot, Joe!" he shouted. "We don't want to set off a new slide of debris." He turned to Ranger and pointed up the mountain of rubble. "Go find!"

Find! Ranger went on ahead. He could move over the heaps of steel and cinder blocks more quickly than Tom. Ranger had done lots of agility training with Luke and Dad when he

was practicing to be a search-and-rescue dog. They'd gone to a junkyard kind of place, with planks and barrels and wooden spools. Ranger had learned to climb slanted boards. He'd learned to relax his feet and spread his toes so he wouldn't slip. He'd practiced climbing up playground slides, through tangled rolls of fencing, and over slippery car hoods. He'd walked over seesaws and swaying bridges. He'd learned what to do when something moved under his paws — not to jump but to slow down, get low, and wait for it to stop.

This field of rubble was much bigger than the practice place. Here, every step felt danger-ous and hot and unsteady, but Ranger knew he could do it. He could go where he was needed.

"Search here!" Tom called, pointing to an area where smoke rose up from the pile.

Ranger walked along a narrow beam until

he got to the spot. With every careful step, he sniffed the air. Mostly, he smelled smoke. But when he stepped off the beam onto a pile of cement and twisted furniture, there was something else, too. It wasn't what he was supposed to find, though.

Ranger had only trained to find people who were alive. But here, he caught a different, sad scent. People who hadn't survived.

Ranger lowered his tail. He didn't bark to alert, but he stopped for a moment and tipped his head until Tom noticed and gave a sad nod.

"We need a crew over here!" Tom called out. "I think he's found remains."

While workers moved hunks of metal and concrete, Ranger kept searching. He picked up the sad, quiet person smell over and over. But never the flowery smell of Risha's mom. When Ranger finished searching an area, he'd come back to Tom. Tom would pet him and say,

"Good job, boy." But his rough hand felt heavier and heavier on Ranger's head.

"K-9! Over here!" someone shouted. And Ranger searched. But again, he found nothing.

Ranger's head felt heavy, and his tail drooped. How could he do his job when it felt like there was no one to save?

Chapter 13

A VOICE FROM THE DARKNESS

"Over here, dog!" someone called, and Ranger set out for another spot on the pile. Building frames towered over him, with jagged tops and blown-out windows. Ranger's paws hurt. His fur was matted with dust. But he knew he couldn't give up. He had to keep searching for Tom's friends and Risha's mother.

The sun was high in the sky when Ranger finally caught a trace of person smell. He followed the scent trail over a pile of beams and charred carpet pieces.

There! The smell was coming from a wide, dark space between two beams.

Ranger barked.

He made his way closer and barked again to alert Tom.

Right away, a firefighter popped up from the opening.

"Good job, boy!" he called. He hugged Ranger and gave him a nice, long neck scratch. Ranger looked back at Tom.

"Good dog!" Tom called. "You found Joe!"

Ranger wagged his tail, but he knew Joe wasn't who he was supposed to find. Joe was doing what Luke used to when they practiced. He was hiding just so Ranger could find him. Still, Ranger let Joe scratch his neck a little more. Tom and Joe seemed happy that he'd found someone, at least.

"Let's get you some water," Tom said. He

started to lead Ranger off the pile, but another rescue worker called to them.

"K-9! Over here!" she shouted, so Ranger went. He circled the area she'd been pointing to, sniffing the air. She was right. There was a person here, but not one who had survived. Ranger dropped his tail and paused for a few seconds.

"We've got one," the woman called to someone. She bent and patted Ranger's head with a sigh. "Good job, dog."

It happened over and over, every time Tom tried to take Ranger off the pile for a break. Other workers would see them and call out.

"Over here!"

"Check here!"

Ranger wanted to help. He wanted to find everyone, if there was anyone left to find. But mostly he wanted to find Risha's mom. He wanted to bring her back to Risha and Max so they could all go home. Maybe then Ranger could go home, too.

But finally, Ranger's nose was so full of the stinging dust that he couldn't smell anymore. Tom saw him panting and said, "That's it. You need a rest."

He walked Ranger off the pile and down the street to a tent where people had set up a sort of hospital for the search-and-rescue dogs who had come with their handlers to help. A border collie named Bella was having her paw bandaged, while a German shepherd named Anna waited to see the vet.

A kind woman with a ponytail gave Ranger a long drink of cool water. She washed his paws in a bucket and rinsed the dust out of his eyes and nose.

"There you go," she said, stroking the wet fur on his neck. "That's a good job you did today."

When Ranger headed back up the street with Tom, almost everyone stopped to pet him. Police officers and rescue workers and firefighters with sad, tired eyes. Some of them hugged him for a long, long time. One firefighter buried his face in Ranger's neck and cried.

When Ranger went places with Luke at home, people always liked him. But here, they *needed* him. He nuzzled every hand that reached out to him. He stayed the longest with people who seemed the saddest.

"Good dog," Tom said, bending down to pet him after everyone else had finally moved on. "You want to go back to work?"

Ranger didn't want to go back at all. It was awful, finding people he couldn't save. But maybe there was still someone he could help. He knew he had to try.

"Can we get a dog here?" a tall firefighter

shouted from atop a pile of concrete. "Joe heard something, but it may have just been more settling!"

Ranger trotted ahead of Tom. He climbed the mountain of rubble.

The firefighter pointed into a dark crevice next to a crumpled staircase. "Search here!"

Ranger lowered his head and sniffed. He smelled all the same things — fire and metal and concrete dust. But there was something else, too.

Ranger couldn't fit down into the space. It was blocked with pieces of building and twisted steel. He pawed at a chunk of concrete.

"He might have something!" the firefighter shouted. Joe and Tom rushed over. Ranger backed away so they could pull some of the heavy pieces from the heap. When they'd opened it up a little more, Ranger leaned in again. With his back feet on a thin railing, he crept deeper into the space, sniffing the air.

There!

It was a person smell! A living person who smelled like dust and smoke . . . and flowers. The same flowers he'd smelled on Risha's scarf.

Ranger barked. There was a muffled thump from below.

Ranger pawed at a chunk of concrete. He barked again, and a quiet voice rose up from the dark.

"I'm here . . ."

"He's got a survivor!" Tom shouted, and more firefighters came running.

"We're here!" Tom called into the darkness. "Hang on! We're going to get you out!"

A Race against Time

More and more rescue workers arrived. They brought axes and crowbars and big metal jaws for cutting away steel beams.

The fur on Ranger's neck prickled. The debris kept shifting under his feet. The firefighters couldn't feel it, but Ranger could. The whole pile was moving and shifting under them. It felt trembly and unstable. Not safe!

But they'd finally found someone to save. No one was leaving now. It felt as if the whole world were holding its breath.

Working together, four men managed to

move the huge beam that was blocking their way. Slowly and carefully, they lowered themselves into the darkness.

"She's all right!" one of them shouted up.

Ranger couldn't stay back. He walked to the edge of the opening and looked down. The flower smell from the scarf was strong, and now Ranger could see Risha's mother! The firefighters were helping her to stand. Two other rescue workers leaned way down and lifted her into the light. Her purple dress was torn and charred, and her hair and face were covered with the sticky gray dust. She blinked at the bright sun, squinted across the pile of rubble to the street, and stumbled forward. "My daughter and her friend . . ."

A firefighter grabbed her arm to catch her. "We'll find them," he said, and eased her onto a stretcher. "But first we need to get you to an ambulance."

Together, the rescue workers carried Risha's mom over the mountain of rubble. When they reached the street, a team of doctors swooped in to help. While they were checking her over and giving her water, Ranger took off down the sidewalk. He had to find Risha and Max.

Ranger could still smell smoke from the towers, but soon there were new scents. River and boat fuel and people. So many people! They were huddled together on the riverbank, waiting. Boats of all sizes came to shore and went away again, loaded with people. The whole river was full of boats, ferrying people away from the disaster. Were Risha and Max still here?

Ranger hurried into the crowd. He wandered through little groups of people standing together. He kept walking, kept sniffing the air until . . .

There!

Ranger caught the Risha smell. He followed it to a pier where she and Max were just about to get on a little tugboat. Ranger ran up to her and barked.

Risha whirled around. "Dog!" Had the dog found her mother? She was afraid to hope, but she had to find out.

She turned to Max's father, who had made his way to the river to find them. "This is the dog that was with us. We have to go with him now!" she blurted out. "I think he's found my mom."

"You coming?" the tugboat captain called out.

Max's father frowned. He looked at Risha. Then he looked back at the boat and shook his head. "Not yet."

Risha kept her hand on Ranger's neck as they hurried back up the street. Max held her other hand, and she was grateful. If they didn't find her mother, she'd need the whole world to hold her up.

"This area is restricted!" a police officer shouted as they turned onto West Street.

"Wait here . . ." Max's father said. He walked up to the officer and talked quietly with him for a moment. He pointed back to Risha and Max and Ranger. The officer's eyes grew wide. He waved them forward and led them up West Street to an area with doctors and nurses and ambulances. They wove their way through a long line of rescue vehicles until Risha caught a glimpse of purple.

"Mom!" Risha ran ahead, dropped her backpack, and climbed into the back of the ambulance, right into her mother's arms.

Tears made muddy streaks down her mom's face. "Oh, thank God!" she said, and buried her face in Risha's hair. "You found me."

One of the firefighters turned to Max's dad. "She was one of the last ones down," he said. "She was almost out when the tower fell.

Somehow she managed to be in the one spot that didn't collapse. One of the search dogs found her."

"This one," Risha said, pointing to Ranger. She hadn't been there when he found her mom, but she knew. She climbed down from the ambulance and hugged Ranger around his neck. She took off her mom's scarf. "Here . . . I don't know who you belong to, but you can keep this." She tied it around Ranger's neck like a bandanna and squeezed him again. "Thank you, dog."

Ranger leaned into the hug. He breathed in Risha's warm smell. Smoke and sweat and the flowery mom smell from her scarf. And then he heard a quiet hum.

Ranger turned and saw Risha's backpack on the street. When Risha climbed back up to be with her mom, he crept quietly over to the backpack. It was halfway unzipped. He pawed at it until it opened, and his first aid kit slid out onto the street.

Ranger looked down at the old metal box. Then he looked out at the mountain of rubble. There was more work to be done here. So much more, and so much sadness. But there was nothing else Ranger could do. His job was done. It was time to go home.

Ranger looked up at Risha hugging her mom in the ambulance, and at Max standing close beside his dad. It felt good to see them together, and safe.

The humming was louder now — loud enough to drown out the sounds of fire trucks and cranes and shouting rescue workers. Light spilled from the cracks in the old metal box. Ranger lowered his head and nuzzled the leather strap around his neck. The box grew warm at his throat as the light grew brighter and brighter. Brighter than the sun that still shone through the smoke and dust. It was so bright that Ranger had to close his eyes.

When he opened them, he saw Luke at the kitchen door with a bowl of chili.

Chapter 15

HOME

"Hey, Ranger!" Luke said, leaning into the mudroom. "Dad put a little extra ground beef in a bowl for you."

Ranger lowered his neck and let the first aid kit drop into his dog bed. Then he looked at Luke and wagged his tail.

"Hey, what's that?" Luke asked. He put his chili down on the shoe bench and pulled the scarf from Ranger's neck. "Where'd you get this? Have Sadie and Noreen been dressing you up in Mom's stuff again?"

Ranger barked. He took the scarf gently in his teeth and pulled it back from Luke.

Luke laughed. "Okay, but if Mom gets mad, you have to tell her I'm not the one who gave you that." He picked up his chili and headed back to the kitchen. "Don't forget there's meat when you're hungry!"

Ranger liked ground beef. But before he went to the kitchen, he took Risha's scarf to his dog bed. He pawed his blanket aside to uncover his treasures — all the things he'd been given on his other adventures. There was an important paper full of words from Walt, the young man on the war-torn beach. There was another scarf — a purple one from Clare, the girl in the hurricane — and a funny-shaped leaf from Marcus, the boy from the big, loud arena far away. Ranger dropped the new scarf into the bed beside them.

He'd miss Risha and Max. They'd been such

good friends to each other and to him. But they were safe with their parents. Ranger had done his job. He'd helped as much as he could. And for now, his work was through.

Ranger pushed his blanket around until all his treasures were hidden again. Then he walked to the kitchen door and sniffed the air.

It smelled like Luke and sizzling meat and chili spices and home.

AUTHOR'S NOTE:

This is the eleventh Ranger in Time book, and it was one of the most difficult to write because I remember the morning of September 11, 2001, so well. My daughter was just over a month old, and I was home with her when my husband called and told me to turn on the television. I watched in horror at what was happening until I couldn't watch any more. Then I went outside and sat with my daughter by the lake, trying to imagine how the world could ever feel all right again.

When my son came home from kindergarten, my husband and I told him what had happened. We explained that terrorists had hijacked four airplanes. That they'd flown three of them into buildings, killing almost three thousand people. That the passengers and crew had heroically struggled to take back the fourth plane, which ended up crashing into a field in Pennsylvania.

But mostly, we told our son about the helpers. We told him about the brave firefighters who had gone into the Twin Towers to rescue people trapped on high floors. We told him about the people who worked in those towers, how they cared for and helped one another that morning, so that many thousands more were able to escape. We told him how so many people are working every day to make the world better and safer and kinder.

The characters in this story are fictional, but they were inspired by the real office workers, police officers, firefighters, rescue crews, and other New York City residents who came together on that day. And it wasn't just people who helped out. An estimated 250–300 search-and-rescue dogs were called to work after the 9/11 attacks. They came from all over the country to assist in search and recovery efforts. Sadly, only twenty survivors were pulled from the rubble of the World Trade Center, most in the first few hours after the towers fell.

After September 12, there were no more people to rescue. Instead, the dogs helped workers recover the bodies of those who had died in the attack. They also served as therapy dogs for rescue workers, firefighters, police officers, and families around the scene. Search-and-rescue dog handlers who spent time at the World Trade Center site talked about how patient their dogs were, how every tired worker who needed a snuggle got one.

Immediately after the attacks, people began planning a memorial. They knew that the world would need a place to come and remember what had happened and to honor those who lost their lives. Ten years later, the National September 11 Memorial and Museum opened to the public at the World Trade Center site. Israeli architect Michael

Arad designed the memorial — two reflecting pools where the Twin Towers once stood, surrounded by trees. The names of the victims of the attacks are inscribed in the stone around the pools.

The World Trade Center site also includes an extensive museum with exhibits on what happened on September 11, the days leading up to the attack, and its aftermath. It includes

objects that tell the story of what happened that day — shoes and eyeglasses found on the sidewalk, and rescue vehicles that were destroyed when the towers collapsed.

This fire truck from New York City's Ladder Company 3 was parked on West Street, near Vesey Street. Eleven members of this fire station died in the collapse of the North Tower.

This staircase is the one that led from the World Trade Center Plaza to adjacent Vesey Street. It's called the Survivors' Stairs now, because so many people used these battered steps to escape.

At the center of the museum's main gallery is the last column to be removed from the World Trade Center site at the end of the cleanup effort in May 2002. Rescue workers,

first responders, volunteers, and relatives of victims signed the column and left mementos of the people they lost there.

Perhaps more than anything, the museum shares stories of courage and compassion from a terrible day in history. There are stories of rescue workers who climbed into the smoke to help people and neighbors who invited strangers into their homes. Stories of a city that came together after an unspeakable tragedy to lift one another up.

FURTHER READING:

If you'd like to read more about the 9/11 attacks, rescue efforts, and search-and-rescue dogs, look for the following books:

10 True Tales: Heroes of 9/11 by Allan Zullo (Scholastic, 2011).

Fireboat: The Heroic Adventures of the John J. Harvey by Maira Kalman (Penguin, 2002).

America Is Under Attack: September 11, 2001: The Day the Towers Fell by Don Brown (Square Fish, 2014).

I Survived the Attacks of September 11, 2001 by Lauren Tarshis (Scholastic, 2012).

Sniffer Dogs: How Dogs (and Their Noses) Save the World by Nancy Castaldo (HMH Books, 2014).

SOURCES:

I'm grateful to the staff of the National September 11 Memorial and Museum for answering my questions and especially to North Tower survivor Wendy Lanski, who talked with me about her experience escaping from the twenty-ninth floor on the morning of September 11, 2001, and served as an early reader for this story. The following resources were also helpful:

Bauer, Nona Kilgore. *Dog Heroes of September 11th: A Tribute to America's Search and Rescue Dogs.* Allenhurst, NJ: Kennel Club Books, 2006.

Dwyer, Jim, and Flynn, Kevin. *102 Minutes: The Unforgettable Story of the Fight to Survive Inside the Twin Towers.* New York: Times Books, 2005.

Gerritsen, Resi, and Haak, Ruud. *K9 Search and Rescue: A Manual for Training the Natural Way.* Edmonton, Alberta: Dog Training Press, 2014.

Hammond, Shirley M. *Training the Disaster Search Dog.* Wenatchee, WA: Dogwise Publishing, 2006.

Murphy, Dean E. *September 11: An Oral History.* New York: Doubleday, 2002.

National Commission on Terrorist Attacks. *The 9/11 Commission Report: Final Report of the National Commission on Terrorist Attacks upon the United States.* New York: W. W. Norton & Company, 2004.

New York Times. "Accounts From the North Tower." May 26, 2002, https://www.nytimes.com/2002/05/26/nyregion/accounts-from-the-north-tower.html.

9/11 The Filmmakers' Commemorative Edition.

Directed by James Hanlon, Rob Klug, Gédéon Naudet, and Jules Naudet, performance by Tony Benatatos, Jamal Braithwaite, and Steve Buscemi. Paramount, 2002.

ABOUT THE AUTHOR

Kate Messner is the author of *Breakout*; *The Seventh Wish*; *All the Answers*; *The Brilliant Fall of Gianna Z.*, recipient of the E. B. White Read Aloud Award for Older Readers; *Capture the Flag*, a Crystal Kite Award winner; *Over and Under the Snow*, a *New York Times* Notable Children's Book; and the Ranger in Time and Marty McGuire chapter book series. A former middle-school English teacher, Kate lives on Lake Champlain with her family and loves reading, walking in the woods, and traveling. Visit her online at katemessner.com.

DON'T MISS RANGER'S NEXT ADVENTURE!

Ranger travels back to 1941 Hawaii, where World War II is on everyone's minds. That includes Ben Hansen, a young sailor stationed at Pearl Harbor, and twins Paul and Grace Yamada, who are making their weekly market trip when Japanese bombs begin to fall from the sky. As the surprise attack puts all of Ranger's new friends in danger, his search-and-rescue training kicks into high gear. Can he help them survive against all odds? Turn the page for a sneak peek!

Chapter 1

READY FOR BATTLE

December 5, 1941

Ben Hansen looked out over the Hawaiian shoreline from the seat of a Kingfisher sea plane. Back home in Minnesota, December meant ice, snow, and air so cold it took your breath away. But here at Pearl Harbor, nearly every day was sunny. In less than a year, the island of Oahu had come to feel like home — but with much more pleasant weather!

Ben loved looking out at Pearl Harbor, where the U.S. Navy's Pacific Fleet was stationed — more than a hundred vessels, including eight huge battleships. He loved the flurry of activity along the docks of Battleship Row. He loved the sparkling Pacific Ocean and the gentle winds that rustled the palm trees of nearby Waikiki Beach. That's where he'd spend his day off tomorrow.

For now, though, there was work to do. Ben checked his instruments and sent an update to the pilot in the front seat. Ben was a radioman who flew scouting missions along with the Kingfisher pilots. They'd launch from their battleship, the *USS Arizona*, and soar over the Pacific.

It was Ben's job to navigate and communicate with the ship. He took care of all the electronics on the plane, too. When it was time to return to the *USS Arizona*, the sea plane would land in the waves and maneuver into position. Ben would need to grab a hook dangling from the battleship's big crane, and he had to be fast!

Sometimes the waves threatened to tip him into the sea. But Ben was an expert with the hook. He'd snatch it out of the air and attach it to the plane so the crane could lift them back onto the ship.

Today, there was no need for that. The *USS Arizona* was in the harbor, so instead of landing at sea, the Kingfisher touched down on the runway at Ford Island.

"Got plans for your day of liberty tomorrow?" Ben asked Tom, the plane's pilot, as they headed back to the ship.

"Going into Honolulu to buy a Christmas gift for my girl back home," said Tom.

"I want to find something nice for my mother and sisters," Ben said. His two younger sisters lived with his mother, a librarian, back in St. Paul. They both had blonde hair and freckles, like he did. Ben's father had died a long time ago, when he was very small, so his mother worked hard to take care of the family. As soon as he turned seventeen, Ben had signed up for the navy so he could help out. And he had to admit, he had done it for the travel, too. He'd always wanted to see some of the faraway places he'd read about in the stories his mother had shared.

Each night before Ben went to sleep in his hammock, he'd take out a poem he kept tucked in his pocket. His mother had copied it onto a card for him and laminated it so it would last longer. The poem was from Ben's favorite book, *When We Were Very Young*. His mother had read it every night when he was growing up.

"Little boy kneels at the foot of the bed,
Droops on the little hands little gold head.
"Hush! Hush! Whisper who dares!
Christopher Robin is saying his prayers."

Ben held the poem in his hands. The words, penned in his mother's handwriting, made her feel closer. He still read them to himself every night before he went to sleep.

After breakfast the next morning, Ben took a small boat to shore with some friends and caught a ride into town. It was December sixth — less than twenty days until Christmas! He couldn't decide on gifts for his family, but he bought some cards to write and send home.

Ben and the other servicemen had lunch at the Black Cat Cafe. Ben brought along a rubber spider he'd picked up at the general store and dropped it on his friend Jerry's hamburger while he wasn't looking. The poor guy jumped about a mile when he saw it. But then he laughed.

"Every day is April Fools' Day when your name is Ben Hansen," Jerry said.

After lunch, Ben and his friends split up. Jerry and Chow were in the *USS Arizona*'s band.

Jerry was an ace at clarinet. Chow (short for Chowhound, because he loved to eat) was the best French horn player around. They wanted to be early for the Battle of the Bands at Bloch Arena that night. Everyone would be there! But Ben and his other friends took a few more hours to enjoy the beach. They stretched out in the sand and rode the waves until the sun sank low in the sky.

They caught a ride back to Pearl Harbor in time to hear the bands. Ben didn't play an instrument, but he loved tapping his feet the music. He hummed along to "There'll Be Some Changes Made" and "Georgia on My Mind." At the end of the night, he watched the jitterbug contest. A little girl who'd come to see the bands with her father stole the show, dancing with a sailor from the *USS Tennessee*.

It was after midnight when Ben got back to the ship and climbed into his hammock. He'd be back on duty in the morning. Even on free days, it was hard to forget the fleet's mission in Hawaii. President Roosevelt had sent them here because of threats from Japan. Some people were even saying the Japanese might attack the fleet!

The rumors made Ben wonder. The American Navy was the best of the best. They were skilled. They were well trained. They were prepared for anything. Ben couldn't imagine the Japanese would dare to think about an attack. But if they did, he and his fellow servicemen would be ready.

Chapter 2

SYMBOL OF THE RISING SUN

December 7, 1941

Paul Yamada squinted into the sun as he pulled on the oars of his family's sixteen-foot rowboat. He made this trip every Sunday, bobbing over the waves of Pearl Harbor to Ford Island to sell eggs from the family's chickens. It was about a mile — a long way to row so early in the morning. Paul was twelve but strong for his age, and so was his twin sister, Grace. He was glad she'd come along to help today. Once they reached Ford Island, they'd load up the pushcart they kept at the dock and go door-to-door with their eggs.

The Yamada family grew vegetables and raised chickens in coops behind their house. It was a lot of work. Paul and Grace had an older sister named Helen who was busy learning to become a nurse. So the work of collecting eggs always fell to Paul and Grace. Each afternoon, they would pick the eggs from the coops, clean them, pack them into boxes, and deliver them to the market.

Paul's and Grace's grandfather, their oji-ichan, had been a farmer back in Japan, where he'd grown up. But farmers struggled there and had to pay high taxes. When he heard that immigrants were being hired in Hawaii, he made the journey across the sea to the island of Oahu.

There, he found work on a sugar planta-tion. He saved and saved his money until he could build the small house where the Yamada family lived today. It was in a neighborhood with many other Japanese American families, including Paul's best friend Jimmy Abe. Jimmy was always game to make stilts out of sticks to race Paul and Grace around the yard. When they were too tired to stilt-race anymore, they'd sit in the shade and read Captain America comic books. Paul's favorite was the one with Captain America punching Nazi leader Adolf Hitler on the cover.

Paul had heard all about the war in Europe on his father's radio. He knew that Hitler's German army had invaded Poland two years ago, and was storming his way through the rest of Europe. And Paul knew that Japan was also invading other nations. Just five months ago, Japan had seized Indochina. Lately, there had been whispers that Japan might attack the United States. Maybe even here in Hawaii!

MEET RANGER

A time-traveling golden retriever with search-and-rescue training... and a nose for danger!